OREGON

Helen Lepp Friesen

www.av2books.com

Go to **www.av2books.com**,
and enter this book's
unique code.

BOOK CODE

H154517

AV² by Weigl brings you media
enhanced books that support
active learning.

AV² provides enriched content that supplements and complements this book. Weigl's AV² books strive to create inspired learning and engage young minds in a total learning experience.

Your AV² Media Enhanced books come alive with...

Audio
Listen to sections of
the book read aloud.

Video
Watch informative
video clips.

Embedded Weblinks
Gain additional information
for research.

Try This!
Complete activities and
hands-on experiments.

Key Words
Study vocabulary, and
complete a matching
word activity.

Quizzes
Test your knowledge.

Slide Show
View images and
captions, and prepare
a presentation.

... and much, much more!

Published by AV² by Weigl
350 5th Avenue, 59th Floor
New York, NY 10118
Website: www.av2books.com   www.weigl.com

Library of Congress Cataloging-in-Publication Data

Friesen, Helen Lepp, 1961-
 Oregon / Helen Lepp Friesen.
   p. cm. -- (Explore the U.S.A.)
 Audience: Grades K-3.
 Includes bibliographical references and index.
 ISBN 978-1-61913-393-8 (hbk. : alk. paper)
 1. Oregon--Juvenile literature. I. Title.
 F876.3.F75 2013
 979.5--dc23

                              2012015936

Printed in the United States of America in North Mankato, Minnesota
1 2 3 4 5 6 7 8 9   16 15 14 13 12

052012
WEP040512

Project Coordinator: Karen Durrie
Art Director: Terry Paulhus

Weigl acknowledges Getty Images as the primary
image supplier for this title.

OREGON

Contents

3

This is Oregon.
It is called The Beaver State.
Beavers were important to the people
of Oregon many years ago.

6

This is the shape of Oregon. It is in the west part of the United States. Four states border Oregon.

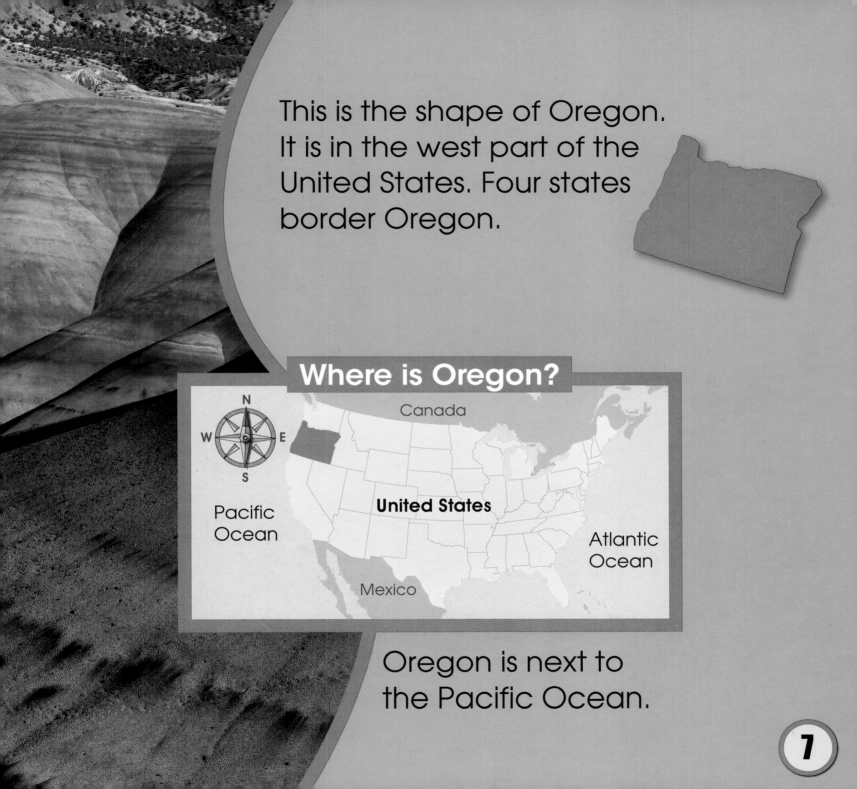

Where is Oregon?

Canada

N
W   E
S

Pacific
Ocean

United States

Atlantic
Ocean

Mexico

Oregon is next to the Pacific Ocean.

Pioneers came to Oregon in wagons. They rode about 2,000 miles on the Oregon Trail.

Many pioneers came from the east coast of the United States.

The Oregon grape is the state flower. It has berries in the fall.

The Oregon state seal has a wagon, ships, and the Sun.

The seal shows the Sun setting over the ocean.

This is the state flag of Oregon.
The back of the flag
has a beaver.

Front

Back

Oregon is the only state
with pictures on both sides
of its flag.

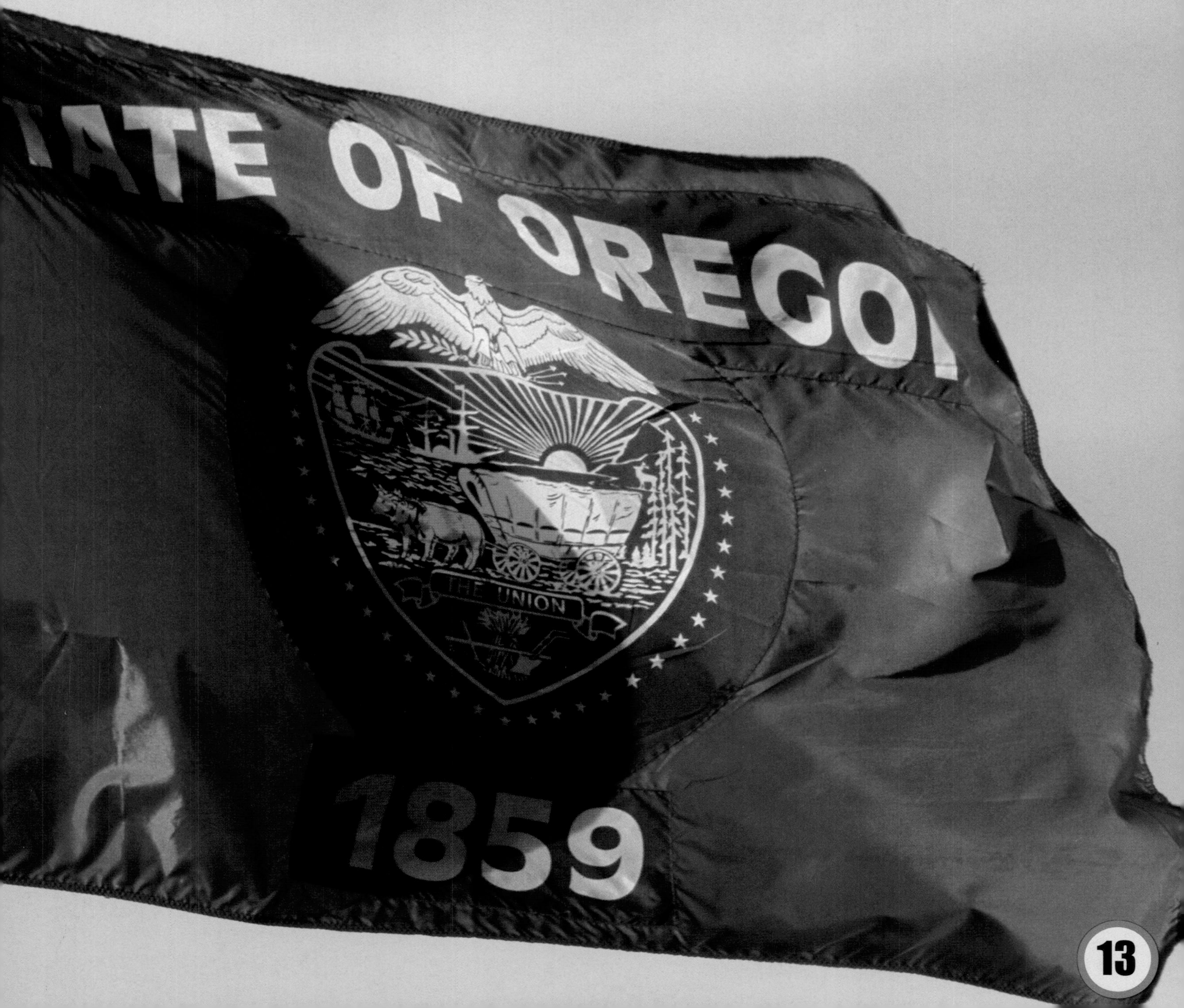

TATE OF OREGON
THE UNION
1859

The beaver is the Oregon state animal. A beaver can steer with its tail. It builds its home under water.

Beavers live in streams and rivers in Oregon.

This is the state capital of Oregon. It is called Salem. Salem is in the middle of the Willamette Valley.

The Willamette Valley is known for the many kinds of fruit that grow there.

Oregon trees are used to make lumber. Lumber is used to build things such as houses. Oregon has 30 million acres of forest.

Almost half of Oregon is made up of forest.

Oregon has beautiful beaches, lakes, and mountains.

People visit Oregon to hike, bike, and look at sea life in ocean tide pools.

OREGON FACTS

These pages provide detailed information that expands on the interesting facts found in the book. These pages are intended to be used by adults as a learning support to help young readers round out their knowledge of each state in the *Explore the U.S.A.* series.

Pages 4–5

American Indians and early settlers in Oregon hunted beaver for food and pelts. In the 1800s, beaver coats and hats were so popular that the beaver almost became extinct. Beavers were so important to Oregon's history that roads, buildings, and sports teams have been named after the animal. The beaver became the official state animal of Oregon in 1969.

Pages 6–7

On February 14, 1859, Oregon became the 33rd state to join the United States. It is located in a region called the Pacific Northwest. Steep cliffs make up Oregon's coast. The west part of the state has mountains and rain forests. Oregon is bordered by Washington to the north, Idaho to the east, and Nevada and California to the south.

Pages 8–9

In the 1840s, settlers traveled to Oregon from several eastern states. Some people traveled by ship, but most went by wagon. The east-to-west wagon route the settlers used was called the Oregon Trail. It was a trail first used by American Indians. The trail was later expanded in the early 1800s by fur traders and trappers traveling on foot and horseback.

Pages 10–11

The Oregon grape became the official state flower in 1899. It has yellow flowers in the summer and berries in the fall. The plant is native to the Pacific Northwest. The 33 stars on the seal stand for Oregon as the 33rd state. The seal also has a setting sun over the Pacific Ocean. This represents the end of British rule in the United States.

Pages 12–13

The state flag was approved in 1925. The flag appears in the official state colors of blue and gold. On the face of the flag is part of the state seal that shows mountains, forests, elk, and a covered wagon pulled by a team of oxen. The year 1859 commemorates the year Oregon achieved statehood.

Pages 14–15

The beaver is the largest rodent in North America. Beavers can be up to 4 feet (1.2 meters) long and 65 pounds (30 kilograms). They cut down trees to make dams to make ponds. Beavers then build homes, or lodges, in the pond. The water protects beavers from predators. Since beavers find food in the water, their homes are near their food source.

Pages 16–17

About 155,000 people live in Salem. The city is in the Willamette Valley, which has rich soil and ideal conditions for farming. Fruits and vegetables, such as apples, peaches, cherries, onions, and cauliflower, grow in the valley. The American Indian name for Salem is *Chemeketa*, which means "meeting place" or "resting place."

Pages 18–19

Oregon is the top lumber producer in the United States, with 18 percent of the country's softwood production. Oregon was the first state to introduce forest management and protection laws. The fishing industry is also important in Oregon. People fish shrimp, crab, and salmon.

Pages 20–21

Oregon has more than 300 miles (483 kilometers) of coastline. Its rocky shores leave many tidepools visible at low tide. These pools teem with life such as sea anemones, crabs, and sea stars. People come from around the world to hike and climb in Oregon's beautiful mountains. Oregon is known as the Pacific Wonderland.

KEY WORDS

Research has shown that as much as 65 percent of all written material published in English is made up of 300 words. These 300 words cannot be taught using pictures or learned by sounding them out. They must be recognized by sight. This book contains 62 common sight words to help young readers improve their reading fluency and comprehension. This book also teaches young readers several important content words, such as proper nouns. These words are paired with pictures to aid in learning and improve understanding.

Page	Sight Words First Appearance
4	important, is, it, many, of, people, state, the, this, to, were, years
7	four, in, next, part, where
8	about, came, from, miles, on, they
11	a, and, has, over
12	back, both, its, only, pictures, sides, with
15	animal, can, home, under, water
16	for, grow, kinds, that, there
19	almost, are, as, houses, live, made, make, rivers, such, things, trees, up, used
20	at, life, look, mountains, sea

Page	Content Words First Appearance
4	beaver, Oregon
7	Pacific Ocean, shape, United States
8	Oregon Trail, pioneers, wagons
11	berries, fall, flower, grape, seal, ships, Sun
12	flag
15	streams, tail
16	capital, fruit, middle, Salem, Willamette Valley
19	acres, forest, half, lumber
20	beaches, lakes, ocean tide pools